# Amelia
## the Singing
## Fairy

For Emma Kneller, a very special
friend of the fairies!

North Tyneside Libraries

Special thanks to

TYN

Sue Mongredien

3 8012 01786 9695

| Askews & Holts | 17-Jun-2011 |
| --- | --- |
| Y M | £3.99 |
| | |

ORCHARD BOOKS
338 Euston Road, London NW1 3BH
Orchard Books Australia
Level 17/207 Kent Street, Sydney, NSW 2000
A Paperback Original

First published in 2011 by Orchard Books

HiT entertainment

A CIP catalogue record for this book is available
from the British Library.

ISBN 978 1 40831 291 9

3 5 7 9 10 8 6 4 2

Printed in Great Britain

The paper and board used in this paperback are natural recyclable
products made from wood grown in sustainable forests. The
manufacturing processes conform to the environmental regulations
of the country of origin.

Orchard Books is a division of Hachette Children's Books,
an Hachette UK company

www.hachette.co.uk

# Amelia
## the Singing
## Fairy

by Daisy Meadows

ORCHARD BOOKS

www.rainbowmagic.co.uk

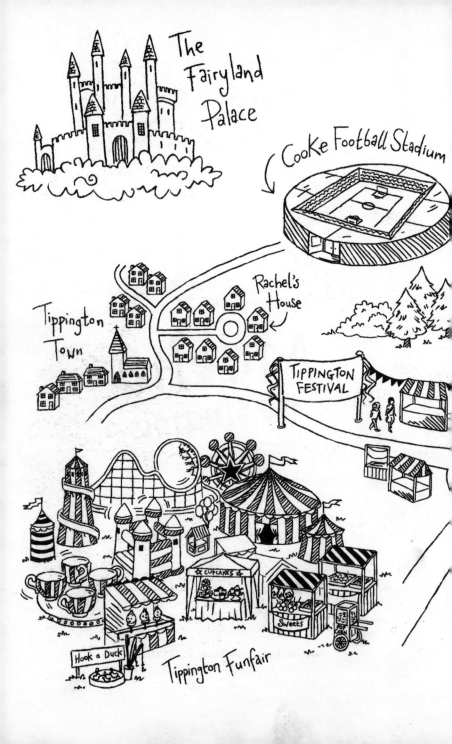

Who likes talent shows? Not me!
So, goblins, listen carefully,
Each Showtime Fairy has a star,
Their magic glitters near and far.

Now do exactly as I say,
And steal these magical stars away,
Then, when our wicked work is done,
We can spoil all showtime fun!

# Contents

## Festival Surprises

WELCOME TO TIPPINGTON FESTIVAL!

WELCOME TO TIPPINGTON
FESTIVAL! Kirsty Tate and her best
friend, Rachel Walker, admired the
large banner marking the entrance to
the festival site. Kirsty was staying with
Rachel's family during half-term, and
the two girls were having a very exciting
time so far. But then again, exciting
things *always* seemed to happen when
Kirsty and Rachel got together!

"This looks great," Kirsty said, gazing around. There were all sorts of food and craft stalls along the sides of the plaza, as well as dancers, singers and jugglers performing in different areas.

"Look at the fountain!" Rachel said, pointing to where jets of water shot up from an ornate white stone base in the centre of the square.

Colourful lights
played across the
falling water
so that the
jets of water
appeared
to be
shimmering
every colour
of the rainbow.

"It almost looks
magical, doesn't it?"
Rachel's dad said, and the
two girls gave each other a
secret smile. Kirsty and Rachel
knew all about magic! Ever since
they'd first met one another, they had
found themselves having all sorts of very
special magical adventures together.

This week they had been helping the
Showtime Fairies on a brand-new
mission to find the magic stars that
belonged at the ends of the fairies'
wands. These stars had the power
to bring out fairies' and
people's talents and
skills, but mean Jack
Frost had ordered
his goblin servants
to steal the stars
and hide them.
The goblins were
now in the human
world, causing lots
of trouble with the
fairies' magic stars.

Kirsty, Rachel and Mr and Mrs
Walker strolled through the festival site.

"Oh, that's where the singing auditions will take place," Mrs Walker said, pointing out a stage at the far end of the plaza. "Are any of your school friends taking part, Rachel?"

"Yes," Rachel replied. "The whole choir's entering. Fingers crossed for Tippington School!" Kirsty held up her crossed fingers too.

Over the last few days, local schools had been auditioning in different categories, including magic, drama, acrobatics and dance. Today, the singing auditions would take place.

13

The winner of each audition went through to a Variety Show at the end of the week, which was being held to raise money to buy new equipment for Tippington's Oval Park. Kirsty and Rachel had really enjoyed watching the auditions so far, but they hadn't always run smoothly. Because the Showtime Fairies' magic stars weren't in their proper places at the ends of the fairies' wands, people weren't performing as well as they should have done. And even worse, the goblins kept turning up at the auditions to take part, causing chaos!

So far, Kirsty and Rachel had managed to get four of the magic stars back from the goblins and give them back to the Showtime Fairies. But there were still three stars to find.

"Oh!" Kirsty was so lost in thoughts of naughty goblins and magic stars that she almost walked straight into a golden statue of a princess. Then she nearly jumped out of her skin as the princess statue slowly bowed her head towards Kirsty.

Rachel's parents laughed at the looks of surprise on both girls' faces. "Aha!" Mr Walker said. "It's one of those living statues. Realistic, isn't it?"

15

"Yes," Kirsty said, recovering herself
and laughing too. She could see now
that the princess 'statue' was actually
a person whose face, body and clothes
were completely covered in sparkling
gold paint. "That's really cool."

Rachel took a coin from her purse and
dropped it into the princess's hat that lay
in front of her, with a hand-written sign
saying 'Thank you'. The
princess turned stiffly and
rather mechanically,
as if she wasn't really
human, then
put her hands
together in a
praying gesture,
and bowed
slightly to Rachel.

"Look, there's another statue over there," Mrs Walker said. "It's a silver knight. Oh, and a red pirate statue as well. Aren't they good?"

The four of them walked further into the festival, and Rachel noticed a trailer slightly to one side. A sign with 'Suzy Soprano' hung from the door. "Wow," Rachel said. "Suzy Soprano! She's really famous, isn't she? She must be one of the judges for the singing auditions."

Kirsty felt excited. This festival was getting better and better! Although it would be even better if they could find another of the missing magic stars, of course... She crossed her fingers again. How she hoped that she and Rachel would be in for another of their amazing fairy adventures today!

# Fairy Cake!

"I think you two girls are going to have lots of fun here," Mr Walker said, smiling at Kirsty and Rachel. "Do you want to have a look round on your own for a bit, then we can meet you for the singing auditions?"

19

"OK," Rachel said. "See you later!"

Rachel and Kirsty wandered towards a stall selling cupcakes. The cakes had been iced in pretty pastel shades of pink, pale blue, lilac, and mint-green, and were covered in edible glitter decorations that twinkled in the sunlight.

"They're gorgeous," Kirsty said, feeling hungry as she looked at them. "Look, that one's decorated with teeny sugar butterflies. How sweet!"

"And that one's decorated with—"

Rachel began. Then she stopped and stared. Was that a *real* butterfly she'd just seen, flitting between two of the cakes? A smile spread over her face as she looked a little closer and saw that the 'butterfly' she'd spotted was actually a tiny fairy!

She nudged Kirsty excitedly. "It's Amelia the Singing Fairy!" she hissed.

Kirsty beamed as Amelia peeped out from behind a cake. Amelia had wavy blonde hair with a pink rose fastened in it at one side. She wore a long sparkly dress, and a pendant with a musical note around her neck.

"Hello!" whispered Kirsty. "Nice to see you again!" She and Rachel had met all seven of the Showtime Fairies when they'd been magically whisked away to Fairyland on the first day of their holiday. Glancing around to check the coast was clear, Kirsty held the top of her bag wide open and Amelia fluttered quickly inside. Then the two girls went to find a quiet spot behind one of the fountains where they could talk to their new fairy friend.

Once there, Amelia flew out of Kirsty's bag to perch on the stone edge of the fountain. "Hello again, girls," she said, her voice tinkling like tiny bells. "I have a strong sense that my magic star is somewhere at this festival. Will you help me look for it?"

"Of course," Rachel said. "We'd love to. Have you seen any goblins around, Amelia? They've turned up to the other auditions this week so they might well be here today."

"They've been pretending they're from a school called 'Icy Towers'," Kirsty added.

Amelia shook her head. "I haven't seen them," she said. "But I haven't had a proper look around the festival yet. Shall we start searching?"

"Yes, let's," Rachel replied. "The auditions are meant to start soon, so if we can find the goblins before then, that would be perfect."

Amelia fluttered back into Kirsty's bag, and the girls set off around the square.

After a short while, they heard some catchy music, and saw some boys wearing matching suits and trilby hats singing along to a portable CD player.

"They're good," Amelia said, peeping over the edge of Kirsty's bag. "Let's go and listen."

A small crowd had gathered around the boy band, and people were throwing money into an open guitar case that was propped up in front of them. Rachel spotted a couple of her friends from the Tippington School

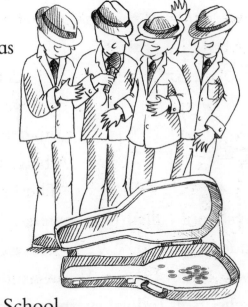

Choir, Libby and Marcus, in the crowd, and went to say hello.

Libby was looking anxious. "This band – Thrillz and Chillz – are really good," she said. "Much better than us. And they're taking part in the singing auditions later. There's no way our choir will beat them!"

"They're from a school called Icy Towers," Marcus added glumly. "We're never going to win against them. We were hopeless in rehearsals today, everyone forgot their words and some people couldn't even remember the tune."

Rachel and Kirsty exchanged glances.
Thrillz and Chillz? Icy Towers? The
boy band *had* to be goblins! They took
a closer look at the band to see that
yes, their trilby hats were pulled low
over their faces to hide their green skin
and pointy noses, and their feet looked
enormous and suspiciously goblin-sized
in their shiny shoes.

"I'm sure you'll be fine," Rachel tried to reassure her friends. Really, she knew that their rehearsals had gone badly because Amelia's magic star wasn't in its usual place at the end of her wand. She was also certain that the goblins sounded better than they normally would because they must have Amelia's star close by, and its talent powers were making them sing extra well.

Kirsty meanwhile was tapping her foot to the jaunty music as the goblins took it in turns to sing into their big microphone. And then she stopped in shock as she realised just what was stuck to the microphone – Amelia's magic star!

# Rachel Has a Plan

Kirsty nudged Rachel and pointed at the star, and Rachel's eyes lit up. She said goodbye to Libby and Marcus and wished them luck, then both girls walked a short distance from the goblin band so they could talk without being overheard.

Amelia was very excited at
the news her star had been
spotted, and
flew right out
of Kirsty's
bag to twirl
around
in mid-air.
"Hurrah!" she
cried, her hair
flipping out around
her as she spun. "Now we just need
to think of a way to get my star back
again, and I can make sure the singing
auditions go perfectly."

Kirsty thought hard. "It's not going
to be easy, getting the star from right
under the goblins' noses," she murmured.
"Have you got any ideas, Rachel?"

Rachel beamed.
A great idea
had just
popped into
her head!
"Amelia,
would you
be able to use
some fairy magic

to make me look like one of the singers
in the band?" she asked. "Because if so,
I can join them, and then, when it's my
turn to sing into the microphone, I can
easily unstick the magic star!"

Amelia smiled. "Fantastic!" she said.
"Of course I can make you look like one
of the band. Let's find somewhere quiet
so that I can work my magic without
being seen."

Kirsty, Rachel and Amelia went behind a candyfloss stand, and Amelia waved her wand. Rainbow-coloured fairy dust poured out from its tip, swirling all around Rachel with glittering sparkles of light. When the sparkles had vanished, Kirsty grinned. Her friend looked just like one of the goblins now, in a suit, hat and shiny shoes.

"Perfect," she said with a giggle. "Go for it, Rachel!" Kirsty and Amelia watched as Rachel strolled up to the singing goblins and stood right next to one of them.

34

Rachel smiled out at the crowd but inside, her heart was beating very fast. If the goblins suspected for one second that she was here to take Amelia's star, they would not be happy! She had to convince them that she was a goblin, or things could get nasty.

The goblins were still singing with gusto, passing the microphone to each other in turn. It was only when the microphone was passed into Rachel's hand that she realised she didn't have a clue what song this was, let alone what the words were!

"Um...*twinkle, twinkle, little star*," she warbled in desperation, trying to keep vaguely in tune with the music. Meanwhile, she was busily trying to unpeel Amelia's 'little star' from where it had been stuck to the microphone! "*How I wonder what you are...*"

"Those aren't the words!" the goblin next to Rachel snapped, and snatched the microphone away. He noticed that the star had come loose on the microphone where Rachel had been unpicking it, and took it off.

Then, to Rachel's dismay, he put the
star safely in the guitar case and snapped
it tightly shut, before
continuing the song.
Rachel could
only pull an
anguished face
at Kirsty and
Amelia in the
crowd. The
plan hadn't
worked!

The goblins' song finished, and the
crowd clapped and cheered. "We'll be
starring in the singing auditions later if
you want to come along and support
us," one of the goblins said into the
microphone. "Thank you very much,
you've been a wonderful audience!"

Just then, an announcement came over the tannoy system. "Good morning, ladies and gentlemen, we hope you are enjoying the Tippington Festival! Just a reminder that our singing auditions will be starting soon, and you're all very welcome to come along and listen. Could contestants make their way to the stage now, please? Thank you."

The goblins began packing up their music and belongings very quickly. "We're going to win this audition hands down," one of them said, high-fiving a friend.

"Um… I'll see you there," Rachel told the goblins, wanting to keep up her disguise. "I've just got to…um…get something."

Feeling disappointed, she slipped into the crowd to find Kirsty and Amelia. She'd been so close to getting Amelia's star – it was frustrating not to have it!

"Never mind," Kirsty said, seeing her friend's downcast face. "You did your best. We'll just have to think of something else."

The three of them hurried behind the candyfloss stand so that Amelia could turn Rachel back into her ordinary self.

Rachel was glad to be a girl again and gave herself a little shake. "Come on, let's go after those goblins," she said.

"We can't let them win the singing auditions."

Amelia raised her wand a second time. "No, definitely not," she agreed. "I'll turn you both into fairies, then we can all fly. Are you ready? Here goes…"

# Funny Feet

Amelia waved her wand and more rainbow-coloured sparkles billowed out everywhere. Then Kirsty and Rachel felt themselves shrinking smaller and smaller, and becoming lighter and lighter. Within seconds, they were the same size as Amelia, and had their own shimmering fairy wings on their backs!

Smiling happily, Kirsty and Rachel
soared up into the air and followed
Amelia as she skimmed high above
the festival. Flying was so much fun!

"Watch out for the fountains!" Amelia
called, swerving to avoid the fine spray
of water. Kirsty and Rachel did the
same. They knew that getting their
wings wet was dangerous, as it made
them heavy and hard to flap.

Soon they had reached the stage,
which was a raised platform with rows
of seats in front of it. People were
sitting down, and there was an excited,
expectant atmosphere as they waited
for the auditions to begin. The three
judges were already in place at their
table, which was covered in a red
velvet tablecloth in front of the stage.

Amelia beckoned the girls to follow her under the tablecloth while they thought what to do next.

It was rather cave-like and cosy under the table, with three large pairs of feet belonging to the judges there. The fairies would be able to peep out from behind the tablecloth to see what was happening on the stage, which made it a perfect hiding place.

"Good thinking, Amelia," Kirsty whispered with a grin. "Although we'll have to be careful not to be trodden on by the judges' feet." She gestured behind her – and then stared as she realised that the middle pair of feet looked rather strange. "Wait," she hissed to Rachel and Amelia, pointing at the middle judge's feet. "Do those feet look *green* to you?"

Amelia and Rachel turned around to look at the feet. Sure enough, the middle judge had large green feet with warts on them, squashed into a pair of high-heeled strappy sandals.

"They're *goblin* feet!" Amelia realised in horror. "Why is a goblin on the judging panel?"

The fairies crept out of the back of the tablecloth so that they could gaze up at the judge in question. Instead of Suzy Soprano, the famous singer, there was a new judge, dressed in a floral dress and a huge hat, covered in so many flowers that it drooped over her face.

The fairies jumped as this goblin judge spoke into the microphone. "Good morning, Tippington!" she – or rather, he – said in a fake-sounding high-pitched voice. "The bad news is that Suzy Soprano has been taken ill suddenly. The good news is that I'm here instead! I'm Felicia Freeze, and I'm much more famous than Suzy."

Rachel, Kirsty and Amelia exchanged worried glances. Oh no. This wasn't good. With a magic star *and* a goblin on the judging panel, Icy Towers were sure to win the audition!

"Let's see who our first act will be," trilled Felicia, putting her hand into a bag of contestants' names. Rachel noticed a key dangling from Felicia's bracelet and couldn't help wondering what it was for. Felicia pulled out a name from the bag. "First up is… " she began, then dropped the name on the floor. "I don't think so," the fairies heard her mutter under her breath. "She's cheating!"

Kirsty hissed indignantly, as the piece
of paper fell down under the table.

Amelia nodded grimly. "And I bet
I know which act she's going to
announce first," she murmured.

"Ahh, here we are," Felicia went on
brightly. "Our first act today is...the
marvellous Thrillz and Chillz. Ooh! My
favourites. We're all in for a treat now!"

## Felicia's Big Mistake

Amelia let out a groan. "Oh no. I knew it!" she sighed. "We can't let Thrillz and Chillz win this, girls, we just can't!"

The audience clapped politely, and the goblin band came on stage, carrying the guitar case which the three friends guessed still had the magic star inside.

"Come on, let's try and get close to that guitar case," Rachel suggested.

Kirsty and Amelia thought this was a good idea, so they flew out from under the table and around the side of the stage, where there were big speakers set up. The three fairies hid behind a speaker, their hearts thumping with nerves.

The guitar case was close by, but the lid was still shut. How could they manage to open the lid and get the star without the goblins noticing?

The goblins were already lined up at the front of the stage, ready to start singing. The fairy friends had to do something, quick!

"I've thought of a way to distract the goblins so that we can open the guitar case," Kirsty whispered suddenly. "Amelia, can you use your fairy magic to make my voice sound really loud for a few moments?"

"Of course," Amelia said, waving her wand over Kirsty. Bright shimmering streaks of magic swirled around Kirsty.

Kirsty took a deep breath. She hoped
this would work. "It's Thrillz and Chillz,
everybody!" she shouted at the top of
her voice. Amelia's magic made it sound
as if Kirsty's voice was booming out
from the speakers. "Make some noise
for Thrillz and Chillz! Cheer if you love
them, let me hear you scream!"

A huge roaring cheer went up from
the audience…and from
the judging panel too.
Kirsty, Amelia and
Rachel watched
in amazement as
'Felicia Freeze'
jumped up on her
chair, wobbling
in her heels as she
punched the air.

"Go, Thrillz and Chillz, yeah!" she yelled hoarsely, forgetting to put on her high-pitched voice and sounding much gruffer and rougher now. "Woo-hoo! Thrillz and Chillz are gonna WIN!"

There was a shocked silence after Felicia's outburst. The other two judges' heads swivelled round to stare at her. "Felicia, may I remind you that as a judge you are meant to be neutral, not supporting one particular act," one of them said stonily.

"She's an impostor, in league with Icy Towers," the other judge said, looking outraged. "That's cheating!"

The crowd's cheers quickly turned to boos. Then a chant of "Off! Off! Off!" started up, with everyone pointing at the goblins and Felicia.

The other two judges exchanged glances and nodded. "We hereby declare Icy Towers are disqualified from the auditions," one said sternly. "And so is Felicia Freeze. You are dismissed!"

A cheer went up from the audience,
but the goblins groaned in dismay.
"That's not fair!" one of
them moaned.
"We didn't even
get to sing!"
whined another.
Then they
turned on
Felicia. "This is
all your fault!"
they shouted.
In all the
commotion, Kirsty
seized the opportunity to
flick open the latches on the guitar
case, lift the lid and creep inside. There
were lots of coins that the goblins had
collected from their busking earlier...

59

and there, sitting on top of them,
was Amelia's magic star. Hurrah!

But before Kirsty could fly out
with it, she heard the goblins' voices
approaching. "Well, if we can't win
the audition, we'll take our magic star
away," one of them muttered sulkily.
"That way, nobody will be any good,
and everyone will have a rubbish time."

Then the lid of the guitar case
was closed, and Kirsty was
suddenly plunged into
darkness.

She heard the latches snap shut, and then she, the money and the star were all tumbling downwards as the guitar case was picked up and carried away. Kirsty felt herself knocked by the coins as she struggled to turn the right way up again. Where were the goblins taking the guitar case? And how on earth was she going to get out of there?

# Jack Frost to the Rescue!

Meanwhile, Rachel and Amelia had
seen what had happened to Kirsty and
felt equally anxious. They had to stop
the goblins! Rachel thought quickly,
and remembered the living statues
they'd seen earlier, and how the golden
princess had stopped Kirsty in her tracks.

Maybe something similar might bring the goblins to a halt? "Amelia, I've had an idea," she said, working it out in her head as she spoke. "Could you magic me up another disguise, please? This time I want to be a rather special statue…"

She quickly filled Amelia in on her idea and Amelia laughed. "I love it!" she said. "Come on, let's fly fast so that we can get ahead of the goblins and give your plan a try."

The two fairies whizzed through the
air above the festival again, following
the goblins. Felicia had by now thrown
away the high heels and was clumping
along in her – or rather his - bare feet,
along with the singers from
Thrillz and
Chillz.

Once Rachel and Amelia had passed
them, they flew down to land behind
an ice cream stand, where Amelia
turned Rachel back to her human size.

Then, with another wave of her wand,
she cast a magic spell which made
Rachel look just like a statue.
But not any old statue.
With the help of
Amelia's magic,
Rachel looked
exactly like an
icy statue of
Jack Frost!

Rachel
grabbed a paper
bowl from the
ice cream stand,
and stepped out
into the path,
just as the goblins
hurtled around the
corner towards her.

"Whoa!" they gasped, coming to
a sudden halt and staring in horror.
"Is that really *him*?"
one muttered fearfully.
"What's he doing
here?"

Moving in the
same mechanical
way as she'd
seen the golden
princess do,
Rachel held
the paper bowl
out towards
the goblins, and
pointed into it with
her free hand.

"He wants money! Give
him some cash!" the goblins gabbled.

67

"Open the guitar case, quick!"

The goblins scrabbled to open the guitar case, and each scooped up handfuls of coins to put in the ice cream bowl. They were so flustered they didn't notice a very grateful Kirsty fluttering out of the guitar case with Amelia's magic star. Hurrah! Amelia, who was leaning out from her hiding place behind the ice cream stand, spotted Kirsty carrying her star and flew to help her. "Thank you, thank you," she cried happily, using her wand to shrink the star to its usual Fairyland size.

Then she slotted the star back onto her wand, where it shimmered with all the colours of the rainbow. "Perfect!" Amelia sighed. "And just in time for the rest of the singing auditions!"

Seeing them, Rachel, who was still disguised as the Jack Frost statue, pointed a stiff finger towards the festival exit as if ordering the goblins to leave.

"He wants us to go! Come on, quick, let's get out of here," they muttered, and scurried off obediently, not even noticing the magic star was missing as they hastily closed up the guitar case to take with them.

Amelia turned Kirsty and Rachel back into girls and they all smiled at each other. "Well done," Amelia said joyfully, twirling her wand in her hand. "Your quick thinking saved the day. Now there's just one mystery left to solve. What happened to Suzy Soprano?"

"Her trailer's not far from here," Kirsty remembered. "Let's go and investigate."

They hurried towards the trailer, where they could hear a voice calling for help from inside. "Let me out! Let me OUT!"

"That's Suzy Soprano – she's locked in," Rachel realised. "And I bet the key on Felicia's bracelet is the one for her door!"

"I'll let her out," Amelia said, waving her wand again. The girls heard the lock clicking magically back, and they rushed to open the door for the famous singer, while Amelia returned to her hiding place in Kirsty's bag.

"Thank you," said Suzy, stepping out of the trailer and blinking in the sunlight. "The lock must have stuck. Thank goodness you heard me shouting!

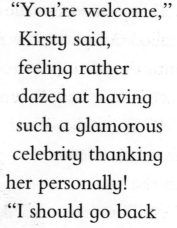

I'd better dash off to the auditions right away."

"You're welcome," Kirsty said, feeling rather dazed at having such a glamorous celebrity thanking her personally!

"I should go back to Fairyland now," Amelia said, flying out of the bag and smiling at both girls. "Thanks so much for all your help. I hope you enjoy the rest of the auditions!"

Rachel and Kirsty watched her fly away, singing to herself, and then made their way to the festival stage, where the auditions were continuing.

As they slid into their seats next to
Rachel's parents, the Tippington School
Choir came onto the stage. "This song is
called 'Magic in the Air'," said Marcus
into the microphone, and the music
swelled behind the choir.

Kirsty grinned at
Rachel. Magic
in the air?
Well, that
was certainly
true! And
as the
Tippington
children began
singing beautifully,
she and Rachel were both sure that
Amelia's talent magic was now working
perfectly once more – and just in time!

Now it's time for Kirsty and Rachel
to help...

## Isla the Ice Star Fairy

Read on for a sneak peek...

## Slipping and Sliding

"Only one day left before the Variety
Show!" Kirsty exclaimed. She and
Rachel were inside Tippington Ice
Rink, gazing at the perfect, gleaming
circle of ice surrounded by rows of seats.
"It's been *so* exciting watching all the
auditions, hasn't it, Rachel?"

Rachel nodded. It was the half-term
holiday and all local schools, including
Rachel's, had been taking part in
auditions for magic, drama, acrobatics,

dance, and singing. The best acts would be performing in the Tippington Variety Show at the end of the week. Everyone was hoping that the show would raise enough money to build an adventure playground, a bandstand and an outdoor theatre in the town's Oval Park. Now it was the final day of auditions, and a pair of ice-skaters would be chosen to take part in the show tomorrow.

"I'm really glad I invited you to stay this week, Kirsty," Rachel said with a smile. "Having a wonderful fairy adventure just wouldn't be the same without *you*..."

**Read Isla the Ice Star Fairy
to find out what adventures are in store for
Kirsty and Rachel!**

# Meet the
# Showtime Fairies

**Collect them all to find out how Kirsty and
Rachel help their magical friends to save
the Tippington Variety Show!**

# www.rainbowmagicbooks.co.uk

Meet the fairies, play games
and get sneak peeks at
the latest books!

www.rainbowmagicbooks.co.uk

www.rainbowmagic.com

There's fairy fun for everyone at
www.rainbowmagicbooks.co.uk.
You'll find great activities, competitions, stories and
fairy profiles, and also a special newsletter.

# Competition!

If you study these four pictures of Isla the Ice Star Fairy very carefully you'll see that one of them is slightly different from the others. Can you work out which one is the odd one out? Make a note of the name of this book and the letter and when you have enjoyed all seven books in the Showtime Fairies series, send the answers in to us!

A

B

C

D

We will put all of the correct entries into a draw and select one winner to receive a special **Rainbow Magic Showtime Fairies Pack** featuring lots of treats!

Enter online now at

# www.rainbowmagicbooks.co.uk

# Meet the Princess Fairies

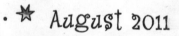

### August 2011

**Honor the Happy Days Fairy**
978-1-40831-293-3

**Demi the Dressing-up Fairy**
978-1-40831-294-0

**Anya the Cuddly Creatures Fairy**
978-1-40831-295-7

### October 2011

**Elisa the Adventure Fairy**
978-1-40831-296-4

**Lizzie the Sweet Treats Fairy**
978-1-40831-297-1

**Maddie the Playtime Fairy**
978-1-40831-298-8

**Eva the Enchanted Ball Fairy**
978-1-40831-299-5